# My "n" Sound Box®

WRITTEN BY JANE BELK MONCURE • ILLUSTRATED BY REBECCA THORNBURGH

Published by The Child's World®
1980 Lookout Drive • Mankato, MN 56003-1705
800-599-READ • www.childsworld.com

ISBN HARDCOVER: 9781503823174
ISBN PAPERBACK: 9781503831391
LCCN: 2017960363

Printed in the United States of America
PA02371

## A NOTE TO PARENTS AND EDUCATORS:

Magic moon machines and five fat frogs are just a few of the fun things you can share with children by reading books with them. Reading aloud helps children in so many ways! It introduces them to new words, motivates them to develop their own reading skills, and expands their attention span and listening abilities. So it's important to find time each day to share a book or two . . . or three!

As you read with young children, you can help develop their understanding of how print works by talking about the parts of the book—the cover, the title, the illustrations, and the words that tell the story. As you read, use your finger to point to each word, modeling a gentle sweep from left to right.

Simple word games help develop important prereading skills, including an understanding of rhyme and alliteration (when words share the same beginning sound, such as "six" and "sand"). Try playing with words from a book you've just shared: "What other words start with the same sound as moon?" "Cat and hat, do those words rhyme?" The possibilities are endless—and so are the rewards!

# My "n" Sound Box®

Little  had a box. "I will find things

that begin with my **n** sound," she said.

"I will put them into my sound box."

Little  found a tree with nuts on it.

Little  climbed the tree. She picked nuts. How many nuts?

Little  counted nine nuts.

She made the number nine.

Did she put the nuts and the number 9 nine into her box? She did.

Next, Little  made nine groups of nuts. How many nuts in all?

Little  counted ninety nuts.

She made the number ninety.

She put these nuts into her box with the

other nuts. Now how many nuts did she

have? Little counted ninety-nine nuts.

She made the number ninety-nine. Did she put the number ninety-nine into her box? She did.

Then Little  climbed

the tree again.

Little  found nightingales.

She found nine nightingales eating nuts!

When the nightingales saw Little ,

they flew into their nests.

Little  put the nightingales and their nests into her box. She was careful because there were eggs in the nests.

Little  could not count how many.

Little 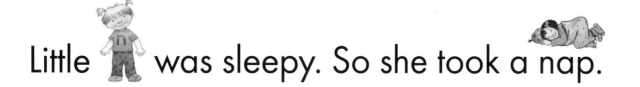 was sleepy. So she took a nap.

The next day, Little  got out her piggy bank.

She emptied out her nickels.
99
There were ninety-nine nickels!

Little  took her nickels to a store. She bought a necklace for her mother and a necktie for her father. She also bought a nutcracker.

Little  had nineteen nickels left. So she bought a nightgown for herself.

Little carried all her new things home. She put on her new nightgown.

Then she heard a noise. She looked into her  box and saw nineteen new nightingales.

They were crying for nuts!

"Don't cry," said Little . "I have enough nuts for all of you." She cracked some nuts.

While the nightingales ate, she

spread out her new things.

# Little n 's Word List

nap

necklace

necktie

nest

nickel

nightgown

nightingale

nine

nineteen

ninety

ninety-nine

numbers

nut

nutcracker

# Other Words with Little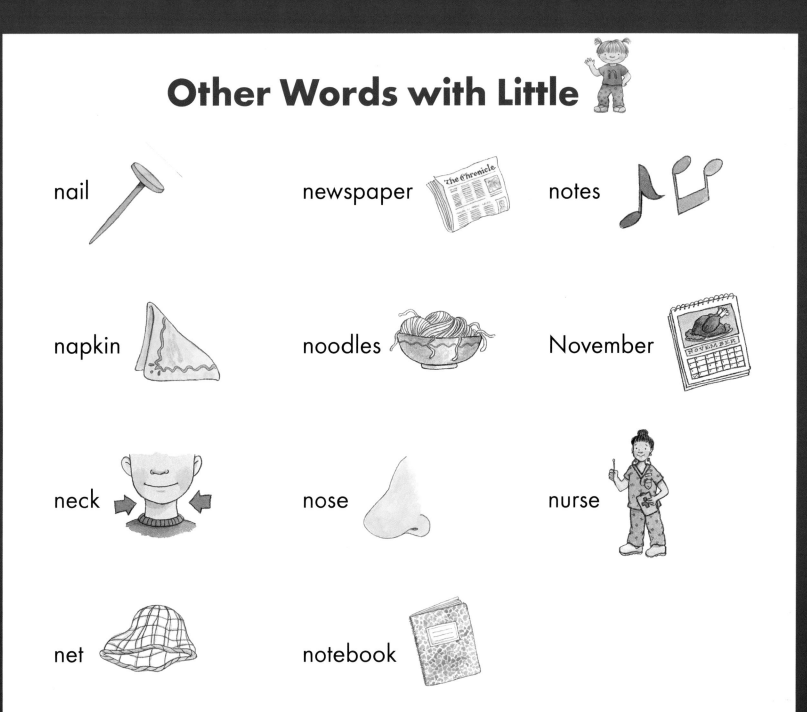

nail

newspaper

notes

napkin

noodles

November

neck

nose

nurse

net

notebook

# About the Author

Best-selling author Jane Belk Moncure (1926–2013) wrote more than 300 books throughout her teaching and writing career. After earning a master's degree in early childhood education from Columbia University, she became one of the pioneers in that field. In 1956, she helped form the Virginia Association for Early Childhood Education, which established the first statewide standards for teachers of young children.

Inspired by her work in the classroom, Mrs. Moncure's books became standards in primary education, and her name was recognized across the country. Her success was reflected not only in her books' popularity with parents, children, and educators, but also by numerous awards, including the 1984 C. S. Lewis Gold Medal Award.

# About the Illustrator

Rebecca Thornburgh lives in a pleasantly spooky old house in Philadelphia. If she's not at her drawing table, she's reading—or singing with her band, called Reckless Amateurs. Rebecca has one husband, two daughters, and two silly dogs.

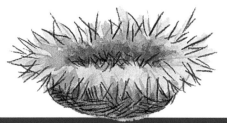